WALKING THE BEAR

For Shameem Ahmed

With thanks to support from a
Society of Authors' Foundation Grant

First published 2013 by Walker Books Ltd
87 Vauxhall Walk, London SE11 5HJ

2 4 6 8 10 9 7 5 3

Text © 2013 by Nicola Davies
Illustration © 2013 by Annabel Wright

This book has been typeset in ITC Usherwood

Printed and bound in Great Britain by Clays Ltd, St Ives plc

British Library Cataloguing in Publication Data:
a catalogue record for this book is
available from the British Library

ISBN 978-1-4063-4089-1

www.walker.co.uk

WALKING THE BEAR

NICOLA DAVIES

with illustrations by
**ANNABEL
WRIGHT**

WALKER
BOOKS

Chapter One

Zaki had perfected the technique of carrying a full pot on his head, so he could practise his flute at the same time as fetching water. But today his fingers kept making mistakes and he was glad his only audience was the two bear cubs bowling along at his feet.

He was about to give the melody one more try before he reached the campsite, when the sound of raised voices came through the trees. There was a huge family row going on. His mother and his four sisters were all talking at once, and his father's voice was rumbling like thunder. Zaki often thought of his family as an orchestra, with his mother playing the melody, his sisters accompanying her and his father providing the deep notes of percussion underneath. But now they sounded out of tune, with no one listening or trying to harmonise with anyone else.

He stepped out from the shade of the trees and saw the women of the family lined up opposite his father, Tareef, like two armies ready to do battle. The girls' saris made a rainbow, and his father's broad body and shaggy head made a big dark cloud. Between them stood his father's older brother, Uncle Ifran, his skinny body leaning this way and that with each blast of the argument, like a reed in a wind. Bilqis, the family's old dancing bear, had taken herself to the limit of her rope and was sitting with her back to the humans and her paws over her ears. The cubs drew in close at the sound of raised voices and almost tripped Zaki up.

"Ah!" his father called out, catching sight of Zaki. "Here are the boys!"

Tareef had taken to referring to Zaki and the cubs as "The Boys" because, apart from himself, they were the only males in the household.

"Put that flute away, Zaki," his father ordered, "and stand up for me!"

Zaki knew what the row was about and he didn't want to get involved. He put the water down by his mother's cooking pots and tried to get away. "I've got to feed the cubs, Father," he said. "They're very hungry."

"Don't make excuses." His father's long arm reached out and pulled Zaki close. The cubs whickered anxiously; they were rather afraid of Tareef.

"Your mother is *ordering* me to give up my bears…"

"Not ordering you, husband," Rashma interrupted. "Trying to *discuss*. But you're too much of a hothead for *that*!"

"*Me*, a hothead?" Tareef cried.

Uncle Ifran held up his hands. "Tareef! Rashma!" he said. "Shall we all calm down? Let's sit and have some chai* and behave like humans, not bears."

Tareef growled and Rashma flicked the end of her sari testily over her head.

Zaki caught his twin sister Nazeera's eye. She grinned at him. She understood whose side he'd rather be on.

Everyone sat down as Ifran suggested, in the shade of the big awning. Summer was coming in fast and even this late in the afternoon it was too hot to sit in the sun. Taroob, Zaki's grown-up sister, made the tea. Then everyone sipped politely from their cups. The cubs tried to climb into Zaki's lap, although they were too big to fit, and he kept them quiet by letting them lick the sweet, milky drink from his fingers.

*chai delicious, spicy tea, drunk at all times of the day in India.

"Tareef," Uncle Ifran began, "the government people will pay you for Bilqis and the cubs, as they paid me for my bear. Then we can use both pots of money to start the new business."

"We wouldn't have to travel all the time, Tareef," Rashma broke in, much calmer now, "so the children could go to school and…"

Tareef wasn't going to listen. He jumped to his feet, anger making him seem even taller than he was. "You want me to give up my bears *now*?" he shouted. "On the eve of our most important show in years? Don't you know this family has lived with bears for generations?"

Rashma nodded sadly. "Of course I know, Tareef. But sometimes change must come."

She spoke softly now, but Tareef ignored her. He caught hold of Zaki's shoulders and shook him like a stage prop. "And what of your son?" he exclaimed dramatically. "Grandson of the greatest bear trainer in all India! He was born to perform with bears! This will take away his *future*."

Zaki knew that this was his cue to say how much he wanted to be a bear trainer. But the fact was, he didn't, although he didn't dare tell Tareef that. Zaki glanced sideways at his mother and sisters. *They* knew that what he wanted was to be a musician and to leave the bears to be bears. But a scream from the next-door camp saved him from saying anything at all. It seemed that Bilqis had grown bored and had escaped to go and raid Auntie Salma's well-stocked tent. Now, fat old human and fat old bear were chasing each other round and round, making enough noise to wake the dead!

Tareef took control of Bilqis, pulling sharply on the rope attached to her nose and tapping her head with a stick. Then he took her off for a walk, while Rashma and the girls calmed Auntie Salma down and an uneasy peace descended on the campsite.

The cubs really *were* hungry now. They stood on their hind legs and scrabbled at Zaki's back with their front paws while he prepared their food. Gently, he pushed them down. "Your claws are getting too big for that stuff now!" he told them. But a moment later they were back, wiggling their noses under the edge of his T-shirt and tickling his skin with their snuffles.

At five months old the cubs weren't bottle-fed any more, but they still needed their milk. Zaki mixed milk from the family goats with dalia* in two bowls and put them on the ground at exactly the same time. If he put one bowl down before the other, then Lallu, who was the greedier of the two cubs, would get to it first, and Bijli, the feistier one, would jump on his brother and start a fight.

Zaki had grown up with bears. His people, the Kalandars, had kept dancing bears for hundreds of years and when he was little almost every family in his community had one. So it felt quite natural that, when his father bought the cubs from a bear dealer when they were tiny, they became Zaki's responsibility. He'd bottle-fed them and cuddled them and spent all his time with them. As far as the cubs were concerned, Zaki was "mother" and they followed

*dalia cracked wheat similar to bulgar.

him everywhere, just as they would have followed their real mum in the wild. He enjoyed this role very much. With so many sisters, Zaki sometimes felt left out and the cubs kept him company.

The problem was that Tareef saw Zaki's caring for the cubs as part of his apprenticeship as bear trainer and part of the bears' apprenticeships as performing animals. And Zaki really, *really* didn't want to follow in his ancestors' footsteps as a keeper of dancing bears. But he didn't dare defy his father. Instead, whenever Tareef suggested that it was time the cubs had their noses pierced to take the training rope, or their big canine teeth removed to make them safe to handle, Zaki found a way to put it off. And whenever he was out of his father's sight, he encouraged his bear-children to be *bears* – to scrabble and dig with their long claws and to poke their curious noses into leaves and soil.

Zaki crouched in front of the cubs as they ate, scratching their necks and watching them. They pursed their lips like a tube to suck up the grains of cracked wheat, and shut their nostrils when the milk splashed and splattered.

"If you were in the forest now," Zaki whispered to the cubs, "you'd be sucking up ants and termites, and keeping the dust out of your noses, just like that."

Zaki sighed. He had protected Bijli and Lallu from having their noses pierced and their teeth taken out for a long time, but he couldn't hold out for ever. Soon his father would insist that it was done. Then the cubs would be trapped in a life they hadn't chosen, just as he was.

Nazeera plonked herself on the ground beside him. She almost bounced. Naz did everything with ten times more energy than anyone else. "Why didn't you speak up when Father asked you what you thought?" she said. "We all know you don't want to train bears. You should tell him."

"There's no point." Zaki sighed. "He'll never let me be a musician and he'll never give up the bears!"

"You're so wrong, Zaki!" Naz exclaimed. "Every

other Kalandar family we know has given up their bear. Father is the last. He has to give in. Keeping bears is illegal now. Father'll have to change and then we'll grab our chance. You can be a famous flute player and I'll be a doctor!"

Zaki shook his head gloomily. "Father will never change. He's going to put ropes through the cubs' noses soon," he said, "and he might as well put a rope through mine too."

Naz shook her head fiercely. "You've got to stick up for yourself, Zaki."

Zaki looked at his sister, her eyes all dancing fire. He sighed. He wished he could be more like her. "I can't," he said. "I just *can't*."

The cubs had finished their meal. They were holding their bowls down with one paw and licking them, their claws clattering against the metal.

"They always do that!" said Naz. "Don't they ever learn that licking doesn't bring the food back?"

Naz began to giggle and her laugh was so infectious that Zaki cheered up in spite of himself.

Chapter Two

Zaki expected the argument about the bears to die down, as it always had before. But this time, it didn't.

The next day, the most important performance in years was to take place. Bilqis was to dance at the birthday celebrations for the baby son of a rich business man, Mr Khan. The walk to his house would take several hours. So everyone was up early, dismantling the camp and getting ready to move.

As Zaki was feeding the cubs, a Land Rover came bumping down the track and across the field. It had writing down the side. Zaki hadn't been to school enough to know what all the words said, but he recognized one of them. It was "bear".

A young man dressed in a dark green shirt and trousers got out and walked towards the family. His name was Mr Ahmed. The family had seen him often and now everyone grew tense, for Mr Ahmed was at the heart of the bear argument.

Tareef stood tall and didn't smile as the man greeted him politely. "Mr Tareef," Mr Ahmed said, "I've come to talk about your bears again."

Tareef folded his arms and said nothing, but the young man was undeterred. "We can help you start a new job," he said encouragingly. "Help send your children to school."

Zaki glanced at Naz; she was holding her breath at the very idea of being able to go to school!

"When has the government ever done anything for the likes of us?" Tareef snapped. "Why should we trust you?"

"Well, my organization is not the government," the young man went on patiently, "and we have helped many Kalandar families, as you know. If you give us your bears, we will care for them and give you money in return. All we want is to help you to find a new livelihood."

"I don't *want* a new livelihood," Tareef replied. "Kalandars have kept dancing bears for generations!"

Mr Ahmed inclined his head respectfully. "I understand, but it is illegal to keep bears now, and soon the police will enforce the law. I don't want you or your family to get in trouble."

Mr Ahmed's face was sad and serious and he held Tareef's gaze for what seemed like a long time.

"All right!" Tareef said at last. "I'll think about it."

Mr Ahmed smiled kindly. "You can find our offices on the Lake Road in town."

Tareef nodded and Mr Ahmed got back into his car and drove away. Then everyone went back to work, without a word, as if the slightest sound might shatter the fragile possibility of Tareef changing his mind.

Mr Kahn's house was very grand indeed, like a huge white cake sitting in a big green garden. Tables were being set out under the trees and lanterns strung in their branches ready for the party to begin. The snooty servant who showed Zaki and his family the little plot where they could camp – well away from the house and outside the garden – told them that over three hundred guests were expected. There would be a parade with a ceremonial elephant and monkeys. Then Bilqis was to dance and "the young master" would ride on her back so as to ensure his future health, good luck and prosperity.

The family made a good team and the camp was soon set up. Although only Tareef, Bilqis and "the boys" were involved in the parade and performance, there were lots of ways in which money could be made from a large crowd. There were charms made of Bilqis' hair, little bear-shaped amulets and all sorts of sweetmeats and snacks to be sold. So Rashma, Salma, Ifran and the girls were soon preparing for business, while Tareef rested in the shade with Bilqis.

With his father snoozing and everyone else busy as a hive of bees, Zaki decided he would take the cubs exploring in the last of the afternoon light. He walked up a sloping field and sat down under a tree. He looked down on the huge house and gardens.

"Imagine being born in a house like that!" he said to the cubs. "I bet Mr Kahn's son could be a musician if he wanted."

But the cubs weren't listening. They were busy snuffling in the leaf litter and digging little experimental holes. Then Bijli gave Lallu a shove and soon they were doing what they liked best – wrestling. So Zaki took out his flute and began to do what he liked best – playing.

He let his fingers do what they wanted, the notes rising into the air without effort, following the tumbling of the cubs. He tried to make the music reflect his thoughts: how the cubs were carefree now, but that soon they'd each have a rope through their nose and have to do what a human told them. But there was so much going on in Zaki's mind that it was hard to make it flow into the music. His fingers stumbled and he stopped playing.

"Hm, shame you stopped," a voice said gruffly. "You're not bad!"

Zaki jumped to his feet in alarm. He spun round and saw an ancient, bearded man, hair on end, beard all straggles, peering at him around the trunk of the tree. The man's eyes were fierce and bright, and he too was holding a beautiful flute painted with a pattern of entwined golden leaves Zaki couldn't take his eyes off it.

"Yes. It's a good instrument," the old man said, replying to Zaki's thoughts. "But only a fine player can play a fine instrument. *You* need more practice, boy. A *lot* more. Work on your breathing. And your *soul*. Not enough *soul* getting into your notes yet. You need to learn to make your mind *quieter*."

And with that, the old man stomped away, towards Mr Kahn's splendid house through the dry stubble of last year's crop.

Zaki watched him go, with his mouth open.

"Zaki! *Zaki!*" Naz's voice sounded rough, as if she had been calling for a long time. Zaki could see her walking up the field edge. She must have been sent to find him, which probably meant he was in trouble.

Chapter Three

The start of the parade had been brought forward by an hour so everyone was in a rush. Tareef threw a bright green shirt at Zaki, together with the collars and leads that the cubs would have to wear in the parade.

"Smarten up, boy!" Tareef growled. "We need to be in position soon."

But Tareef wasn't really cross. Performing always put him in a good mood. Zaki often thought that Bilqis was just his father's excuse for doing what he liked best, which was telling stories and showing off.

As the sun sank behind the trees, all the performers and animals were lined up at the entrance to the garden and the parade began. Two drummers led the way. Behind them walked the elephant, a rather moth-eaten old creature, but still splendid enough in her bejewelled headdress. Her mahout* was a little old and moth-eaten too and struggled

*mahout a person who cares for a working elephant.

to button a ragged gold jacket over his round tummy. Then came a troupe of performing monkeys and their handlers – a family very like Zaki's own who he'd seen before at big events like this. He always thought that the monkeys had faces so clever, so cunning that *they* might be the keepers and the humans their slaves. Then came Tareef in a shining white dhoti* and a waistcoat encrusted with sequins. He held himself very tall and straight and his dark hair spread like a cloud above his solemn, noble-looking face. Bilqis walked on her hind legs beside him, her long fur combed to a glossy shine and a necklace of silver bells around her furry throat. One of Tareef's long, elegant hands held Bilqis' rope, pulling it very slightly upwards so she wouldn't drop down and walk on four feet. She huffed grumpily at the cubs if they got too close, so Zaki was careful to keep a few paces behind. He held their leash in one hand and played the mughli* with the other. The cubs were overawed by it all and stuck close to Zaki's legs.

*dhoti a traditional Indian men's garment, like a sarong.
*mughli a small flute used with a little handheld drum, the damru, by Kalandar bear keepers to announce their arrival.

Following the animals came a flock of child acrobats doing cartwheels and behind them more drummers and musicians. The whole of the parade was wrapped in a confusion of loud, happy noise, as it snaked its way between the cheering guests. Zaki looked among the musicians for the old man, but there was no sign of him, or his beautiful flute.

The sky grew dark and the world became a fairy tale of glowing lanterns and the smiling faces of the party guests. Zaki was happily lost in it all – the confused music, the cheering, the smell of food and woodsmoke. From time to time, he glimpsed Naz, his mother or one or other of his sisters in the crowd, smiling their most charming, businesslike smiles and selling the charms and amulets, sweets and puris*.

The parade reached a ring of flat ground lit with a string of electric lights around it and the show began. The elephant stood, rather unwillingly, on her hind legs and lifted her tubby mahout in her trunk, the monkeys raced and misbehaved to order, making the crowd shriek with laughter and the acrobats leapt and spun as if gravity was just a silly story that someone had made up.

Then it was Tareef's turn. The moment he stepped into the light, the crowd grew quiet. He beat a rhythm on the damru* and Bilqis stepped from one foot to another as she'd been trained to do

*puri a crispy pancake with a spicy filling.
*damru a hand-held drum played by twisting the wrist so that the ball inside strikes the drum skin.

all her life. She was very old now and her stepping was a bit slow and wobbly, but all the same Tareef's black hair and her dark coat made them seem like two different sorts of bear, dancing slowly together. Then Tareef began to tell the story of Bilqis' life as "Queen of the Bears".

"She was the fiercest bear of all time," Tareef told the enraptured audience. "All the animals feared her. The dhole*, the wolf and even the mighty tiger ran from the scourge of her paws."

Of course, it was complete rubbish: Bilqis had been captured as a helpless cub, the same as every other dancing bear. But the audience loved it, especially as Bilqis had been taught to snarl when the rope was pulled in a certain way, and she did this now. Even though she didn't have big canine teeth to show, the crowd jumped. Zaki smiled; he wondered how many of them knew that sloth bears like Bilqis were indeed fierce hunters ... of ants, termites and figs!

The snarl was the cue for Zaki and the cubs to

---

*dhole an Indian wild hunting dog. These are beautiful and very fierce.

make a brief appearance, so that Tareef could tell another bit of the story.

"Once a year, Queen Bilqis returns to her forest kingdom to meet Jambavan* the King of the Bears. And these are their cubs, with the blood of royal bears in their veins."

Zaki made a circuit with the cubs, aware that both he and the little bears were supposed to be looking regal. But the cubs were skittish, and Zaki felt thoroughly uncomfortable in the too-tight, shiny shirt. He was glad when they could move out of the light and let his father take centre stage again.

During the finale, Bilqis walked on all four feet so she could carry small children on her back. The first was the birthday boy, Mr Kahn's son, one year old and fat as a grub. He gurgled and grabbed at Bilqis' fur, pulling it hard. She might have snarled but Tareef kept an especially tight hold on her rope at this point: bitten babies were *not* good business. While Kahn Junior and other small children rode

*Jambavan King of the Bears in Indian myths.

on Bilqis' back, Tareef told how Bilqis "Queen of the Bears" had been persuaded to leave the forest to bring health and good fortune to human babies. The audience cheered wildly and the show came to an end.

Tareef and Bilqis melted into the dark and Zaki was about to follow them when Naz wiggled her way towards him through the throng.

"That famous old flute player you like, whats-hisname," she said breathlessly, "he's playing up near the house. You should go."

"*Jayarman*?" Zaki exclaimed. "*Raju Jayarman*?"

"Yes, that's the one!" Naz said. "Go on, Zaki! I'll take the cubs." She grabbed the cubs' leashes and pushed him away.

"Thanks, Naz." Zaki smiled. "Don't let go of them, not for a second. They'll just run after me!"

On a little stage not far from the terrace, the performance had already begun. Zaki felt the music slithering through the night air and straight into his heart. He recognized the playing of his idol, Raju

Jayarman, at once. He had stood in CD shops for hous listening to his music, until the owners threw him out.

The famous flute player sat on a pile of silken cushions, dressed in a long black jacket, his hair combed, his beard trimmed, playing a flute with a pattern of gold leaves!

Zaki gasped; this was the scruffy old man from under the tree! Which meant that Raju Jayarman had given him advice, *in person*! Had told him he was *not bad*!

Zaki worked his way between the people until he was right at the front of the crowd. The old musician was completely lost in his own playing. Zaki too was in a dream, soaking up the wonder of actually seeing his hero play, right there, close enough to *touch*!

The blissful moment didn't last. There was a series of sudden shrieks from the crowd and two furry missiles shot right across the little stage, brushing the famous man with their fur, then knocking Zaki flying in their delight at finding him.

Raju Jayarman ignored it all and simply went on playing.

Chapter Four

Uncle Ifran did a wonderful job of pacifying Mr Kahn, so the family got paid, but Zaki and Naz were still in a *lot* of trouble.

Zaki and the cubs were banished to sleep under a tree. Meanwhile, the argument about bears broke out again. Rashma argued that as long as the family was dependent on dumb animals, then mishaps like this would go on happening. Tareef argued that it wasn't dumb animals that were the problem, but dumb humans making stupid mistakes.

Zaki curled up with the bears beside him. The quarrel rumbled on like a monsoon storm. All three older sisters – Taroob, Afra and Ushta – were backing their mother now, along with Auntie Salma and Uncle Ifran. But it was no good, Tareef always won in the end, Zaki thought sleepily.

"Zaki! Zaki!" His father's urgent whisper woke him just as it was beginning to get light. "Wake up. I have something for you!"

Zaki sat upright, between the still-sleeping cubs.

"Here!" Tareef said. "It's a present." He handed Zaki a long box tightly wound with cloth and knotted string.

Tareef had never given Zaki a present before and his heart pounded as his sleep-clumsy fingers worried at the knots.

"Do that later!" Tareef told him crossly. "Now, I want you to listen to me!"

Zaki put the parcel aside.

"I've had to give in," Tareef said. "I've never seen your mother so determined. So I'm going to try the taxi-driver thing." Tareef spoke as if the words "taxi driver" tasted bad on his tongue. "Ifran and I can buy a vehicle together," he went on, "with the help from that Ahmed and his lot. I'll have to give them Bilqis to get the money, but she's getting old anyway..."

Zaki couldn't believe what he was hearing! Naz was right. Tareef really *was* going to change. Old Bilqis would have to live in a zoo, but Bijli and Lallu were different. They had never been roped and were still young enough to learn to live in the wild. His bears could be bears and he could be a musician! Zaki's hopes soared like birds, but then he saw the sly twinkle in his father's eye...

"The thing is," Tareef continued, "I may not *like* taxi driving. So you must take the cubs away. Go to my uncle's place, outside Itarsi. It's very quiet – Ahmed and his lot won't find you there. Train them, then when all this silly fuss dies down, we can be back in business!"

Tareef thrust a leather purse into Zaki's hands. "Here's some money to keep you going," he said.

Zaki stared at his father in astonishment. "You want me to go *now*, Father?" he said.

"Yes. Of course," his father said, as if banishing your son was absolutely normal. "Before your mother wakes up."

"But..."

Tareef stood up, an irresistible giant whose will must be obeyed. "No buts, Zaki," he said coldly.

"After the mess you made last night, you owe me respect."

So Tareef planned to go back to bear dancing with two young bears, ready trained by his dutiful son. The present – which was probably some tacky outfit for performing with the bears – was just bribery. Zaki had never been so angry in his life.

"One thing we have to do before you go," said Tareef, "is put the ropes in their noses. I'll get the piercing gear ready now. We can take their teeth out, too."

Once the cubs had their noses pierced and their canines broken, they could never be wild bears. There would be no going back for them, or for him. Zaki must act. It was now or never.

You've got to stick up for yourself.

Naz was right. This time, he was *not* going to do what he was told.

"All right, Father," Zaki said evenly. "You take the piercing equipment into the field, so if the cubs make a fuss we won't wake anyone. I'll join you in a few minutes when I've fed them."

It would take his father a while to get ready. Perhaps just enough time for Zaki and the cubs to make their escape, if he was quick.

Zaki grabbed what he could – his blanket, with the bears' bowls and a bag of dalia, wrapped in it. He shoved the leather money pouch inside his shirt. He almost left his father's bribe behind, but then he picked it up. "I'll sell it!" he told himself bitterly. Then he put the collars and leashes on the bears and dragged them, protesting, into a shambling run.

The trees at the edge of the garden gave them cover until they reached Mr Kahn's long drive. Where the drive met the road, a line of trucks had pulled up so the drivers could get some breakfast from the roadside foodstalls. Zaki pushed in among them, looking for a lift. Truck drivers were often happy to let you ride in the back of a truck, sometimes for free, and sometimes in exchange for a little money. He asked the drivers urgently where they were going. Most of them named places Zaki knew, villages and towns close by that he and his family had visited with the bears. He needed somewhere further away. Then one driver, a young man with shiny black hair combed into a wave, answered his question with a place name Zaki had never heard of.

"It's a village up in the hills," the man said with a friendly grin, "about seven hours' drive from here. I'm delivering a statue."

That sounded perfect! It was a big enough distance to put between Zaki and his father's anger and somewhere that might let the bears be bears.

The young man leant down and whispered in Zaki's ear. "You running away from something?" he asked. "Don't be scared. I ran away too once."

Zaki nodded.

"The name's Daaruk," said the young man. "Always pleased to meet a fellow adventurer. C'mon, let's get out of here!"

Daaruk's truck was ancient, but the peeling paint was pretty, with peacocks painted on the back and coloured patterns down the sides. The huge statue was hidden in its wrapping of sacks and lashed securely to the truck's cab, leaving plenty of space for a boy and two young bears.

But the cubs had never been in any kind of vehicle, let alone one with a sack-covered shape towering over them! They spat and snarled, refusing to get in. Zaki grew anxious, certain that Tareef was about to appear, breathing flames of anger.

"Be cool, little runaway," Daaruk said. "I have the solution." He dived into his cab and pulled out a plastic box. "The finest barfi* this side of Mumbai," he said, and waved the open box towards the cubs. The sweet, sugary smell worked like a charm, tempting the cubs on board. They clambered up with almost no help from Zaki and he climbed up after them.

"Here," said Daaruk, giving Zaki the box. "Take it for them. I'm too fat already." He shut the pea-cock-covered tailgate and they were off, heading down the road with the entrance to Mr Kahn's drive growing smaller and smaller in the distance.

Zaki felt a bubble of relief, quickly followed by a much bigger one of sheer panic! What had he done? He had never even been away from his family before, and here he was defying his father, stealing the cubs and heading off down the road to who knew where. He shut his eyes and squeezed back the hot tears. His father would explode with anger! His mother would worry! And Naz? She

*barfi an Indian sweet, a bit like fudge.

would smile! Zaki took a deep breath: he was doing the right thing, for the cubs and for himself.

Chapter Five

Daaruk stopped for petrol and Zaki used some of his precious store of money to buy more milk for the cubs and some tikkis* for himself. He fed the bears in the shade at the side of the garage, and then it was time to set off in the opposite direction from his uncle's house, his family and everything he'd known before.

"C'mon, little runaway," Daaruk said. "Time to load up your furry friends and get going!" He handed Zaki a paper package. "Here's some pineapple halva* to get them into the back, fast!"

Daaruk was right. The smell of halva worked even better than the barfi. Soon the peacock truck and the bears were heading out of town at top speed.

The movement of the truck made the cubs dozy. They curled up in the shade on a pile of sacks and went to sleep.

Daaruk banged on the back of his cab to attract

*tikki a spicy potato patty.
*halva a kind of sweet.

Zaki's attention. "Come and talk, Runaway!" he shouted over the noise of the engine.

Zaki leant out towards the open window of the cab and found that if he shouted, he could hold a conversation with Daaruk's reflection in the wing mirror.

"What's your plan? Gonna set up as a bear trainer?" Daaruk asked.

"No!" Zaki yelled. "No! That's not what bears were ever meant to do. My cubs are going to live in the wild."

"OK," said Daaruk. "So, you just going to let them go?"

"Ye-ess," Zaki said uncertainly.

"Well," Daaruk said, "I know a good place, but those cubs look like they still need you to be Mummy Bear!"

Zaki didn't answer. He pretended to have dust in his eyes and went to sit beside the sleeping cubs. He had only thought as far as getting away from Tareef and simply letting the bears free. But Daaruk

was right. The cubs wouldn't just run off into the woods! They were too young to manage on their own. He would have to stay with them. His heart beat fast at this thought. He would be away from his family for *weeks*, perhaps even *months* and would have to live in the wild! He couldn't be sure if he felt terrified or exhilarated at the thought of it. At least it might give Tareef time to stop being angry!

At the next stop, Daaruk parked in the shade of a huge tree. The cubs were still sleeping and Zaki didn't want to disturb them, so he decided to stay in the truck.

"Want me to get you anything?" Daaruk asked.

"Well, maybe there are some things I'll need," Zaki said, trying to sound brave, "when I'm with the bears in the forest."

Zaki held out some money.

But Daaruk smiled. "You keep your money, eh?"

He came back to the truck in a short while and handed Zaki a backpack. Inside the pack was a saucepan, a knife, a box of matches, a few candles, a bag of rice, a bag of dhal*, a tin of dried milk and a huge bottle of water.

"Thanks, Daaruk!" Zaki said. "You *must* let me pay you!"

"No way!" Daaruk laughed. "It's good karma. All good deeds come back to you in the end."

After the town, the road grew steep and potholed. Rocky hillsides and knots of trees began to replace the flat hills. Villages were smaller and further apart. The old truck groaned and grumbled, and the cubs slept on, almost as if they understood there was nothing to do but sleep.

At last, after a long climb, they came out onto the flat and Daaruk pulled the truck off the road. He banged on the tailgate and let it down. "OK, little runaway. This is a good place for you to get out."

Zaki looked out over the side of the truck. To his right, the ground fell away in a long slope of tumbled rocks and bushes, with empty fields at the bottom. Ahead and above were more rocky

---

*dhal a tasty stew made of lentils and spices.

hills with patches of woodland in the dips between them, and in the distance the green blur of a bigger forest. There would be ants and termites among the rocks and fruit trees in the woods – wild food for cubs.

"There's a village about six kilometres along the road, but people don't come up here much in the dry season," said Daarut.

That was good too. There would be no one to ask awkward questions about where Zaki was from, and it was important for the cubs to learn to live without people.

Zaki jumped down and coaxed the yawning cubs to follow him. Daaruk closed the tailgate. Once again, fear bubbled up in Zaki's heart. But once again, he saw there was no going back.

"Thanks, Daaruk," he said, even though "thanks" didn't seem like enough.

"That's OK, little runaway." Daaruk's naturally smiley face grew suddenly serious. "I drive this way every month or so. I'll leave you some food behind that rock whenever I pass." He pointed to a big pale boulder with a bush growing out of it. "And I'll wait a little while and honk my horn, so if you need help, you can come and get it."

Zaki nodded. He didn't trust himself to speak. He shook Daaruk's hand and the young driver leapt back into his cab.

"I think you'll be OK," he said, leaning from the window. "D'you know why?"

Zaki shook his head.

"The statue in the back? It's Jambavan, King of the Bears! Pretty sure he's going to protect you." Daaruk honked his horn and pulled away down the dusty track.

Chapter Six

Zaki looked around. The sound of Daaruk's truck had faded into the distance now and there was no more traffic noise, not even a tractor or the sound of cattle bells. Just birds. More birds than he'd ever heard before. Somewhere close by, a peacock shrieked and the cubs' ears swivelled to focus on the sound. The sun was sinking and the hottest part of the day was long gone. Soon it would be night.

"Well," said Zaki, speaking out loud to make himself feel a little braver, "we'd better find somewhere to sleep before it gets dark!"

Up or down, that was his first decision and instinct made it for him: up seemed safer. He shouldered the backpack and began to scramble over the rocks. The cubs were full of energy after their sleep, and surged ahead, their sensitive noses reading the air ahead of them. They pulled on their leashes and Zaki realized that there was no need for such things any more. He undid their collars, stowed them in his pack and set off again.

It felt good to be moving. Climbing up the rocks was fun. He began to feel a little braver. The hill was crowned with a huge boulder, too round and smooth to climb. Zaki and the cubs skirted it and then stood together looking – or in the cubs' case sniffing – out over the far side of the hill. There were no houses or villages to be seen in this direction. Just more rocky hillsides and trees.

Zaki had hoped for a cave of some sort, to offer some solid protection, but looking down below him, he saw something even better: tucked under the lip of the hillside was a small temple. A tree had grown over half of its roof and some of the stonework had crumbled. It had almost blended back into the landscape, but it still had walls and the outline of doors and windows. It was built of pinkish stone that caught the evening light and gleamed. Zaki rushed down the hill towards it, sending stones scudding in front of him and making the cubs pant and uff in their effort to keep up.

The temple was just one room, with a stone floor and a window looking out over the valley. Half the roof had gone, but the tree that had grown over it gave some shelter. There were bits of dried poo around the place, showing that other animals had been there at some time, but they looked pretty old.

Zaki's family were nomads for at least seven months of the year, so he was used to making camp in far worse places than this! He set to work in good spirits. He gathered a bundle of twigs to make a brush and soon had the floor swept clean. He collected rocks to make a little fireplace just outside the front door and then sticks and fallen wood for a fire. He laid out the saucepan ready for cooking. And as he worked, the cubs explored, but never more than a few metres from him, and running close for reassurance every time there was a sudden shriek of a peacock or an unfamiliar scent in the air.

The sun sank towards the horizon and Zaki lit

his fire. He boiled up some rice and lentils in Daa-ruk's saucepan, then mixed some of it with milk and put it in the cubs' bowls.

While Bijli and Lallu ate, Zaki went inside and unpacked, making himself at home. As he unrolled the blanket, out fell his father's package. It made him feel angry all over again. He removed the string and the fabric wrapping. At least they would be useful. But he didn't open the box. Instead, he stood one of Daaruk's candles on it. Huh! It would make a good enough table anyway, whatever nonsense it held.

He took up his old flute and went to sit beside the fire. On the slope below the temple, the cubs were snuffling about, learning their first lessons about the place that would be their home. Above them, the evening sky blushed pink and the first scattering of stars appeared.

You need more practice, boy. A lot more. Work on your breathing. And your soul.

Already, Jayarman's playing and his advice seemed like something from long ago, but Zaki held it in his mind as he began to play.

Only a fine player can play a fine instrument, Jayarman had said.

Zaki sighed. Perhaps, while the cubs learnt to be real bears, he could learn to be worthy of a better instrument...

Chapter Seven

Zaki's eyes snapped open. He got up fast. Bijli and Lallu were on their feet too. In the faint moonlight, he could see their eyes glinting and their long fur on end. Something was at their fire, scratching about. It sounded big ... very big! Zaki imagined a tiger – huge, snarling and ready to eat him and the cubs in one gruesome meal. Then he heard claws scraping at the empty saucepan, then at the nylon of the backpack that held the rest of the rice and dhal. Tigers were not vegetarian! That made Zaki feel braver. Whatever it was must not be allowed to eat their food.

There was no point trying to light a candle; it would blow out as soon as he began to move and anyway there was enough starlight to see his way to the door. Bijli gave a faint growl and tried to get in front of him, but Zaki pushed the cub back as he stepped into the doorway.

The creature was smaller than it sounded – a

low, rounded shape not much bigger than a fat sack of rice. It heard them moving and froze, so for a moment everything was still, with just the hooting of an owl coming from another hilltop.

"Shoo!" Zaki told the animal rather timidly. "Go away!"

It didn't move, but began to rattle like a bundle of bamboo canes given a shake.

Now Zaki knew what it was – a porcupine! It wouldn't eat them, but its sharp quills could be dangerous. Tareef had told him of a bear he'd once owned that had died after being pierced with porcupine quills. So Zaki kept back and stooped to feel for a rock. One well aimed throw would send it running, but as Zaki's fingers closed on a good missile, Bijli shot past him, growling! Zaki grabbed at Bijli's fur with his right hand and threw the rock with his left hand. The rock struck the porcupine and it ran, but not before Bijli's nose had made contact with the animal's spines.

In all his years of living with bears, Zaki had never heard one scream as Bijli did now. He rolled at Zaki's feet, scrabbling at his snout with his front paws. It was too dark to see exactly what had happened and Bijli snarled and struggled when Zaki tried to comfort him!

Zaki wanted to run away or call for help, but there was nowhere to go and no one else to turn to. He took a deep breath. Light. That was the first thing he should do.

He added sticks to the dying fire and stirred it

back to life. The flames leapt up and gave a bright, flickering light. Bijli still cried and Lallu uffed and snorted in fear, but being able to see what was happening made it seem less horrible.

Next, he had to find a way to hold Bijli still, so he could examine his injuries. Zaki fetched his blanket and the roll of tough string that had bound up the present. He threw the blanket over the suffering cub. The little bear fought, but pain was weakening him so it wasn't too difficult to truss him up like a parcel with his head sticking out and his paws firmly tied. Now, Zaki crouched over Bijli, almost sitting on him to keep him still, and tied another strip, torn from the fabric wrapping, around his snout to keep his jaws closed.

It was bad, but not as bad as it could have been. Zaki could see that four spines had pierced the loose fleshy part of the cub's nose and lips on the left side. They stuck out like frozen whiskers. Carefully, he slipped his fingers inside the cub's mouth, feeling for the tips of the porcupine spines poking through on the inside. His father had told him that pulling spines out the way they went in was hard, because they were barbed and tore the skin. Pulling them the way they wanted to go did much less damage.

Ouch! There were the tips all right! Zaki withdrew his fingers and bandaged them with little strips of cloth to protect them. Then, one by one, he pulled the spines through. There was a frightening amount of blood, but Bijli gave up screaming after the first one and lay still, just whimpering from time to time.

Quickly, while Bijli was still partly unconscious, Zaki examined the cub's front paws. Bijli had scrabbled at the spines in his nose and some had snapped off and pierced his paws. The barbed spines had worked their way into the pads and between the toes, but none had gone deep. Most came out with some pulling and pushing and only one had to be cut out with the sharp tip of the hunting knife that Daaruk had put in the backpack.

The nightmare of removing the spines seemed

to go on for hours. When at last it was done, Zaki was surprised to find that it was still night-time and that the dark sky showed that dawn was far away. He was exhausted and very worried about Bijli, who was limp and panting. But there was nothing more he could do. He left the cub wrapped in the blanket so he wouldn't worry at his paws and nose, then curled up with his head on Lallu's furry side. As he fell asleep, Zaki thought that at least the cubs had learned a useful lesson for all wild bears: *keep clear of porcupines!*

Chapter Eight

Lallu woke Zaki by snuffling at his neck. It was early morning. Birdsong sounded like the notes from a sitar, ringing in the cool air, while the sun sat behind the misty blue hills. Bijli was wriggling in his blanket prison with such energy that Zaki was sure the cub must be feeling better. He set Bijli free and the cub gave himself a good shake. He was limping slightly on his left paw and he snarled when Lallu nibbled at his ear, but otherwise he seemed unharmed. Zaki's blanket, however, was bloodstained and had been almost shredded by Bijli's claws. He would have to find something else to sleep on.

The cubs were ravenously hungry. Zaki used the last of the water to mix up dried milk and divided it between the cubs. He needed to find more water very soon and hoped there would be a stream at the bottom of the valley. Before setting off to search, he reused the string from the parcel to sling the bags of rice and dhal from the branches of the roof-tree, to keep them out of the way of any other hungry visitors. He put the plastic bottle in the backpack and led the cubs down the hill.

They made slow progress because of Bijli's limp, but Zaki was glad to go slowly. The ground was steep and treacherous and he didn't want to risk any more injuries. In one particularly steep spot between two rocks, he lost his footing and slid, sending earth and pebbles tumbling down the slope. He put out his hands to stop his slide and was instantly crying out with pain. Ants, big ones, were stinging his bare arms. Zaki slapped them off and was about to move on when he remembered that this could be the cubs' breakfast!

He turned to face the slope and began to hack at the surface with a stick, calling to the cubs. Bijli and Lallu knew about digging. Digging was a good game! They began to scoop at the earth on either side of Zaki, instinctively snuffling at the ants that swarmed out to protect their colony from

attack. But the bears didn't
seem to be eating them. Would
he have to teach them how to do that too?
Then he remembered something that Tareef had
told him.

The mother bear chews the food and lets the cubs eat it from her mouth.

Zaki didn't like the thought of two slobbery cubs licking crushed ants off his tongue, but he could perhaps do *something* to help them realize that ants were their natural food.

Without giving himself any more time to think about it, Zaki put his head close to the ground where the ants raced about in panic and let the insects run over his hand. Ignoring the stinging, he thrust an ant-covered finger into his mouth. As he chewed, the ants crunched and tasted bitter and acidic, like an unripe lemon. But Zaki smacked his lips to show the cubs that this was really the yummiest food you could possibly imagine. He made himself do it twice more, mostly by imagining how much this little scene would make Naz laugh.

Lallu got the hang of ant-eating first: closing his nostrils against the dust, he formed the tube like mouth that he used to eat dalia and milk. Then he breathed out to blow away the dust and sucked up the ants. It must have worked, because he began to chew. Ants, Zaki thought, must just naturally taste good to bears, because Lallu repeated the blow and suck tactic at once. This gave Bijli his cue, but his lips and nose were obviously very sore and he kept getting ants up his nose and having to sneeze them out in a nasty, snotty mass.

By the time the bears had made a hole as big as a car tyre, and the only ants left were a few legless stragglers, the sun had risen above the hills. The bears were panting and Zaki's tongue was so dry that it was sticking to the roof of his mouth. If they didn't find water in the valley, it would be a long and thirsty walk to the village to find a well.

The river at the bottom of the valley looked completely dry. The mud at the edges was baked so hard that it looked like cracked concrete. But the cubs' thirst had sharpened their sense of smell and they ran ahead, weaving between boulders. When Zaki caught up with them, their noses were in a pool, hidden in a deep crack in a rock. As Zaki leant down to try the water himself, he patted the cubs' fur.

"Well done!" he told them. "You found your first wild food and drink!"

In less than a day, Lallu and Bijli were a small step closer to being wild bears.

Chapter Nine

Within a very few days, Zaki and the bears had established a routine. As soon as there was a glimmer of light in the eastern sky, they got up and made their way down the hillside to find water. Other animals were doing the same, so as Zaki and the bears pushed their way through the dry grass and bushes, birds flew up from the pools and, most mornings, monkeys scattered into the trees. These langurs* were timid, very different from the bold creatures Zaki had encountered in towns and villages who would steal food from your plate and washing off the line. The birds' cries and the monkeys' sharp alarm calls echoed in the still morning air. It sounded to Zaki like some of the best music he had ever heard.

They had discovered several pools along the valley. Most were muddy but easy to get to, and fine for the cubs to drink from. Hidden in deep, narrow cracks in the rock were a few pools that could only

---

*langurs monkeys with long legs and tails and pale fur, common in Indian countryside and towns.

be reached if Zaki lowered his bottle down on a string. The reward was water that was clear and fresh. So both he and the bears could start their morning with a drink.

The search for food went on all day and only ended when they returned to the temple at night. They walked for miles, resting for a couple of hours during the hottest part of the day in the shade of trees or in between boulders. They didn't walk a straight path, but zigzagged along and stopped while the cubs dug or sniffed at things, doubling back to find water when they needed it. Zaki brought cooked rice folded in a leaf to keep his hunger away, but he did not share it with the bears. He had decided that it was important that Bijli and Lallu learned to find their own food. Hunger was a good teacher. It encouraged the cubs to investigate everything with their sensitive noses and test things out with teeth and claws.

Ants and termites were getting more difficult to find as the drought drove them deeper and deeper underground, and set the surface of the soil hard. But there were trees with ripe figs: little pink and brown ones, red ones the size of ping-pong balls and pale, fat yellow ones that Zaki knew were gular figs. The bears snuffled up the fallen fruit from the ground and clambered onto low branches to reach ripe fruit that still hung on the trees.

One morning, they found a bael* tree and Zaki almost split his sides laughing as the bears' teeth and claws failed to break open the big hard fruits. The bael fruits rolled like footballs and the cubs got crosser and crosser, but Zaki knew he had to resist the temptation to slice one open with his knife until the cubs had learned to do it for themselves. Bijli's bad temper solved the problem in the end, as he pounded on a fruit with both front paws and a snarl. The fruit split open and in moments Bijli had his nose deep in the juicy pulp inside.

Zaki ate the fruits too, and although wild ones weren't as juicy as those from the market, they were a change from dhal and rice. But he could never eat

*bael tree a medium-sized tree with hard skinned, grapefruit-sized fruit.

the amount of fruit that the cubs did; they ate until their tummies were round.

The cubs had also discovered honey. One afternoon, Lallu had shimmied up a tree and in moments was frantically clawing aside strips of bark and rotten wood. The air filled with furious bees and Zaki had to run to a safe distance, where he lit a wodge of dry grass to surrounded himself with smoke to keep the bees off. Lallu ignored the stings for long enough to rip out crusts of yellow comb, full of honey and fat bee grubs. Some he ate but some simply fell to the ground and Bijli gobbled it up. But in the end, both bears and Zaki had to run fast for several hundred metres to lose the angry bees.

After a beehive, an ant or termite nest had been raided by the bears, it was like an empty plate, but the biggest trees were like a larder that could be visited many times. They provided food for other creatures too – tiny striped squirrels, monkeys and sometimes even chital*, with their big soft eyes

*chital Indian spotted deer, similar to fallow deer.

and lovely spotted coats. At first, the monkeys and deer disappeared as soon as the cubs and Zaki approached, but as they went back to the same trees time after time the animals grew less wary. If Zaki sat back and kept quiet, the deer would sometimes stay and the langurs would climb down from the branches. Then, deer, monkeys and bear cubs would feed within a few metres of each other. This was another good lesson for the cubs. They learned not to get too close to the stags, who were grumpy, aggressive and ready to use their antlers to poke an inquisitive cub in the bottom!

But there was a much more dangerous lesson in store around the fig trees. Late one afternoon, when they had walked further than ever before along the valley, they found a new tree: a huge banyan*, its twining branches falling like a woody waterfall over boulders and rocks, with a carpet of fallen fruit in the shade of its enormous canopy. The cubs had been digging for ants and termites without much success, so they began gobbling up the figs at once.

*banyan a type of fig tree that grows on top of other trees, smothering them with its roots.

Zaki sat with his back against a rock and ate the last of his rice and dhal. Above him in the branches, a troupe of langurs quarrelled and lazed and a little party of parakeets chattered. Light dappled through the leaves and streaked the tall dry grass surrounding the tree. He was just deciding that animals were much more peaceful to be around than his big, noisy family, when the langurs in the branches above him began to make a noise that he'd never heard before: a little run of sharp coughing calls. At once the chital stopped feeding. Their heads shot up on their elegant necks and their big ears and eyes all turned towards the tangled grass on the far side of the tree. At first the cubs took no notice, but soon their noses picked up the scent of danger.

"Uuufff" said Bijli.

"Uufff!" Lallu replied.

The cubs turned and scampered towards Zaki, climbing over him and trying to sit on his back as they had done when they were very little.

Deer, monkeys and now the cubs stared, sniffed

and listened to something … something in the long grass. Zaki strained his eyes, but could see nothing except the chaotic weave of stems and stalks, light and shade. Fear stretched in the air, like a high, tight note.

Everything froze.

Then with the suddenness of a smashed plate, the something exploded into the clearing: a lightning strike of orange and black, a blur of speed that set the deer bounding in panic and the monkeys screaming in terror. It was so fast that the spotted corpse of a chital had been carried back into the cover of the grass before Zaki's mind had time to blaze the word "TIGER!" across his brain.

He had worried about finding food and water, and about getting injured far from help or eating something poisonous, but he hadn't thought about *tigers*, until now.

Zaki sat with the trembling cubs and thought of all the times they had been so busy eating fruit that a tiger could have crept up on them unawares. And now, no matter how much he told himself that there could be only one tiger in the area, and that it was definitely not hungry just now, was hard to make himself come out from the shelter of the rocks. But the light was fading and he knew he must reach the sanctuary of the temple and the comfort of the little fire before dark.

All the way back along the valley, he saw a tiger in every shadow and heard one in every rustle and whisper of the trees.

That night, Zaki built the fire up so it would burn for longer and sat up late staring into the dark, looking for the glint of eyes looking back at him.

He woke lying in the ashes with the cubs snuffling at him, already hungry and thirsty. Behind the now familiar sound of birds and calling langurs there was another sound: the honking horn of a lorry! Zaki sprang up and began to race towards the sound, afraid that Daaruk would leave before he reached the road.

But he needn't have worried. His friend was waiting for him.

Daaruk looked at him and whistled. "OK, so which one of you three bears is really a boy?" he said.

He made Zaki look at himself in the truck's wing

mirror: his hair was a matted bush and his clothes were filthy and covered in bits of leaf and grass.

Zaki grinned at his reflection. He was glad he looked different. Here, with Daaruk, he realized how different he *felt*. The wild bear-life had got inside him.

Running down the hillside towards Daaruk's truck, Zaki had thought that he would ask his friend to take the three of them away from where tigers might eat them. But instead he found he was telling Daaruk about how lucky he felt to have seen a real wild tiger and about the bears' adventures with bees and bael fruit and porcupines and about playing his flute on starry nights.

When at last Daaruk left, he carried with him a list of things Zaki needed to live like a bear for a lot longer.

Chapter Ten

The rains came very late. For a month, clouds gathered on the horizon, thunder rumbled and rain fell in the distance, but not on the temple and its dry rocky hills. For another month, it rained in patches, one day a shower or two and the next dry. The heat was so intense that it drove Zaki and the cubs to rest in the shade for hours in the middle of the day. The cubs slept easily in the most uncomfortable of places, but Zaki was always restless. There had been no sight or sign of the tiger since the day they'd seen the chital killed, but Zaki guessed tigers were pretty good at going unnoticed. So he stayed on the lookout for danger, too wary to play his flute during their midday rests. Sometimes, he thought of his family during these long, hot hours and wodered if Tareef was driving a taxi or if Naz was going to school. But the thoughts carried no weight in his heart, almost as if his life with Rashma, Tareef, Naz and Bilqis belonged to another person altogether.

And while he was thinking these thoughts one day, another lesson pushed itself into the cave where he was resting with the cubs.

The entrance was a gap between two rocks, bright white with midday sun one second and blocked with a dark, shaggy shape the next. It was another sloth bear, the first wild one that they had encountered. It too was looking for a cool place to rest, perhaps a place it had used before, and wasn't expecting to find it occupied. The cubs woke instantly from a deep sleep and scrambled to Zaki's side, with their fur bristling. They had fed well on fruit, insects and honey and they were now more than half-grown, but they weren't big enough to stand up to this bear; it was huge! It had the widest head Zaki had ever seen, and the broadest shoulders. Zaki guessed it was a male. Tareef had told him that male bears will kill cubs that are not their own. He stood up straight and tried to look as big as possible.

The bear took a long sniff and didn't seem to like what he smelt.

"Wa-a-a-a-a!" he said sharply, opening his mouth as if to show that no one had ever taken any of *his* teeth away, and waggling his long lower lip in threat.

Behind them was another, narrower, exit from the cave, which Zaki was pretty sure he and the cubs could fit through, but only one at a time. Zaki

stepped back towards it, pulling the cubs with him and keeping his eye on the big bear. As he did so, his hand found a dead branch wedged between rocks. Fear gave him strength and he wrenched the branch free and held it ready. He backed some more. They must be almost there!

"WA-A-A-AAA!" said the bear again, and rocked forward on his front legs, hair bristling and looking even bigger.

Now! Zaki jabbed at the bear and exploded with the loudest yell he could manage, while the cubs snarled and did some "Wa-a-a"s of their own. The bear was clearly surprised enough to step back. It was all Zaki needed. He pushed Bijli and then Lallu into the narrow gap, jabbed the bear hard with the branch and yelled at it one more time, before wriggling backwards into the hole himself, leaving the branch, its point facing outwards to stop the bear from getting too close. As soon as the three of them had squeezed through the gap, they ran.

Zaki, Bijli and Lallu fled up the hillside over rocks almost too hot to touch, out onto a grassy clearing at the top and straight into more danger! Smoke and the unmistakable crackle of fire. Somewhere close by lightning had hit the ground and lit the tinder-dry grass. On the opposite side of the hill, fire was melting the grass and turning trees into torches.

Zaki was very afraid of fire. He'd seen it race through a settlement of tents and huts in minutes, so his instinct was to turn and run. But that would take them back towards the male bear.

He called the cubs close using the "uff-uff" bear call, not their human names, which he had stopped using anywhere but in his head. Then he took a careful look at the flames. With no wind to drive it, the fire wasn't moving very fast so they could skirt around it and down into the next valley, which would take them, eventually, back to the temple. The smoke would hide their scent in case the bear had thought of following.

Carefully, Zaki and the bears walked along the fire's advancing edge. In front of them, Zaki noticed kites* swooping down and hornbills* hopping, almost into the flames. It was only when Lallu, always quickest to find new things to eat, began crunching at a large cricket that Zaki realized the birds were making use of the opportunity the fire created: hundreds of tiny creatures were fleeing the flames. The kites and hornbills – and now the cubs – had learned that the smell of smoke could mean dinner as well as danger.

*kite a bird of prey with a forked tail.
*hornbill a large fruit-eating bird with a huge horny beak.

Chapter Eleven

The rains came in earnest at last, falling in thick curtains and filling the dry riverbed with a rushing torrent. The cubs' shaggy coats helped to keep them warm and dry, but Zaki often had to seek shelter while the cubs dug for termites or climbed a tree – until Daaruk brought him a large, black umbrella.

Finding food was now much easier. Termites and ants were busy close to the surface of the soil again, and the cubs spent most of their days digging, snuffling and sucking up insects like so much dalia and milk. There were other foods too: Zaki learnt the knack of finding the nests of birds. The cubs enjoyed their eggs raw, but Zaki carried his back to the temple at night to cook them. Soon the cubs could find nests on their own, although termites and ants were still their favourite food.

The cubs grew fast, in size and in confidence. They no longer stuck to Zaki's side but made little expeditions on their own. This made Zaki happy and sad at the same time. He wondered if that was how his own parents felt about him and his sisters: happy to see them growing and learning, sad to think that it meant one day they might leave home.

Every night he took up his flute and played, sometimes for hours, trying to put a little of every day's events and feelings into his playing, always thinking of Jayarman's advice.

Practice ... breathing ... soul...

The bears were becoming real bears and Zaki felt that at last he might be becoming a real flute player.

But Bijli brought Zaki's practising to an end. One night, when the monsoon season was starting to wane, Zaki woke to the sound of crunching. He flicked on the torch that he saved for emergencies. There in its beam was Bijli. The cub had always been fascinated by anything that smelled strongly of Zaki and he had found his flute. In his tiredness that night, Zaki had left it on the floor by mistake and Bijli had chewed it into pieces!

"My flute!" Zaki shouted at the cub. "How will I live without playing?" He screamed and wrenched the remains of the flute from the cub's jaws, hitting him hard on the head with the torch to make him let go. The terrified cub ran out into the night and Zaki was instantly sorry for his anger. He called and called but there was no sign of the cub. At last Zaki lay down to sleep, worried and exhausted. Bijli would come back on his own very soon, he told himself. He would give him rice and milk to say how sorry he was.

But when dawn came, Bijli had not returned. As soon as it was light enough, Zaki set off to search for him. The sky hung low and grey with cloud and a cold lump of fear and remorse lay at the bottom of Zaki's chest as he and Lallu clambered down the steep hillside towards the river.

It didn't take long to find the cub. He must have gone straight to his favourite drinking spot: a flat rock that ran to the edge of a pool. That was where the tiger had found him. It had made a good meal, and there was little left of the cub, just enough to tell Zaki that this was indeed his bear-child.

The muddy ground was torn up with footprints of bear and tiger and there was orange fur under Bijli's claws showing that he had been brave and feisty to the end. Zaki watched Lallu snuffling at what remained of his twin. He pushed at the bloodied fur with his paws, cuffing Bijli's head as if inviting him to wrestle as they had done as little cubs. But when Bijli didn't respond, Lallu began to wander away and there was nothing Zaki could do but follow miserably in the falling rain.

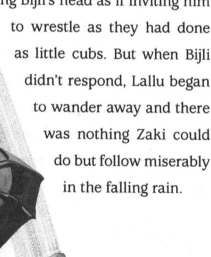

Chapter Twelve

Bad news, they say, seldom travels alone. A few weeks after Bijli's death, Daaruk arrived with some more.

The truck driver sounded his horn as usual and Zaki went down the hill to meet him. Lallu hung back; he'd become wary of all humans but Zaki.

After Daaruk had listened sorrowfully to the news of Bijli's death, he shook his head and said, "I'm sorry, Runaway, but there is more to add to your troubles. A bear has attacked a woman from the village. She tried to chase it from her crops and it turned on her. The villagers are angry. They have seen you here with the bears. They will drive you away and kill the cub."

Zaki hung his head. It was all going wrong. Bijli was dead, his flute was destroyed and now Lallu's life was threatened just as he was becoming a real bear.

"Don't give up, Runaway!" Daaruk pleaded.

"But what can I do?" Zaki cried.

"Leave today. As soon as you can. Go to the National Park!" Daaruk said. "It's four days' walk. Just follow the line of the river!" And he pointed over the temple to the line of blue forested hills in the distance. "Your cub will be safe there and then you can find your way back to your family!"

"Maybe I won't find a way back, Daaruk," Zaki said sadly. "I'm almost a bear myself without my flute to keep me human."

"I could have brought you another!" Daruuk cried.

"No," said Zaki. "Since Bijli … I haven't the heart to play."

They travelled light. A bag of rice, a saucepan and some matches; a blanket and umbrella; a torch. At the last moment, not quite knowing why, Zaki grabbed Tareef's gift, still unopened. Perhaps he did it because he wasn't angry with his father any more, but grateful for all Tareef had taught him about bears – knowledge that had served him well, here in the wild.

Then Zaki and Lallu simply began to walk. As he moved away from the temple, not down the slope towards the river which was their usual route, Lallu hung back. He sniffed the entrance to the temple perhaps taking in some last trace of his brother. Then, with a loud "uff" he turned and hurried after Zaki, almost as if he too was glad to escape the memories.

Zaki guessed that Lallu was well-fed enough for finding food to take a low priority for a few days, until they were at a safer distance from any angry villagers. So instead of their usual slow zigzagging path, they walked straight ahead and the cub seemed to understand that this was a different kind of travelling.

It took less than a day to go further than they had ever been before. They stopped at dusk and Zaki made camp on the top of a huge boulder that gave him a clear view in every direction. Without the walls of the temple around him, he was afraid that he would lose Lallu to the tiger, so he stayed awake all night and kept the fire going. In the morning, they came across a large termite mound and Zaki allowed himself a short sleep, his back against a rock, while Lallu tore open the colony with his claws and sucked up the insects.

As they travelled, Zaki's heart lightened. He was still very sorry for the anger he had shown Bijli, but he remembered what Tareef had said about bear mothers.

It's a very lucky mother that rears both her cubs. One almost always dies. But then the other thrives!

He was right. Without Bijli, Lallu was more alert and independent, which pleased Zaki very much. It showed that Lallu might make it alone.

The tree cover grew more dense as they travelled. Every morning, the birdsong was louder and there were calls that were unfamiliar to Zaki. They saw chital, and for the first time sambar*. Zaki loved to see the deer, but it made him nervous; where

---

*sambar a large deer. This is a favourite food of the tiger.

there was plenty of tiger food, there could be plenty of tigers and leopards too. Each night he took more and more care to choose a campsite, and gathered more and more wood, to be sure of making a big fire. Lallu wanted to be up after dark, hungry after the day's travel, and Zaki had to call "uff uff" for longer and longer every night to get him to come close to the fire, where it was safe.

On the fifth day, the rocky hills gave way to flatter ground and more trees. Zaki felt sure they must be inside the National Park now, but he kept going just to be sure. It was nearly dusk when they came to a place where the ground fell away again and the river went over a waterfall into a deep, clear pool. It was a beautiful place and Zaki couldn't resist scrambling down the rocks and diving in. The water was delicious and Zaki swam in lazy circles and watched Lallu sniffing about on the bank, turning over rocks in search of food.

It was a good place to camp. The waterfall protected them from one direction and the rocks below it were clear of any trees or grasses where a tiger might hide. Zaki built a fire and Lallu found a big dead fish in the shallows and gobbled it up, bones and fins and all, then settled down to rest with a full belly. Zaki ran his fingers through his friend's long fur, stroking the broad place between his ears. The bear's eyes closed in pleasure, and he slept.

Zaki cooked some rice. There was enough for a few more days. After that, he wasn't sure. At least here they were safe from people who might harm his bear. Tired and relaxed from his swim, he too slept. Thunder grumbled in the distance and lightning flashed faintly in the sky. Somewhere far, far away, Zaki thought sleepily, the monsoon had brought one last, late storm.

Cold water over his head. A horrible rushing roar. Eerie grey light. And not a nightmare. Real. *Real.*

Zaki floundered, breathed water, air, water again. He pushed himself to the surface. The distant storm had fallen somewhere upriver and sent a flash flood raging downstream, swelling the water-fall in seconds and washing away Zaki's camp. Logs, leaves, branches floated around him, but not a bear. He forced his mouth above the water.

"Lallu! Laaalluuu!" he shouted. Then, "Uuuff-ufff."

But there was no chance of hearing or being heard above the rushing of the water. The flood slammed him into a rock, knocking him half-sense-less, so he didn't grab hold of it. But the second time it happened, in spite of the pain of impact, he hugged the wet, gritty surface, paddling his feet against it, scrabbling to get a little higher – high enough to see a wet, black shape being swept away too, its nose up above the surface.

Lallu was alive!

Zaki lost his grip. The water sluiced him between the rocks like a fly in a plughole. He was swirled and slammed, pushed under, beaten up. Everything went black.

Like a log he was was washed ashore, and came

to his senses coughing and
spluttering on a little muddy
beach. He pulled himself into a sitting position and
wiped the water and blood out of his eyes. Just a few
feet away, the water still leaped and roared – a flash
flood, ten metres wide and impossible to cross. On
the other side, he could see a line of trees where
the forest came down to the rushing water's edge. A
black shape crawled from the far side of the flood,
stood up, snorted and shook the water from its fur.

Zaki forced himself to his feet, too weak and
hoarse to shout, but he tried anyway. Lallu's ears
were keen; they swivelled round to Zaki's voice the

way they had to the sound of a peacock's call on that first day on the roadside. Lallu looked at him, breathing in Zaki's scent from across the river, a long in-breath that heaved the bear's sides. Then he blinked, breathed out, turned away and walked slowly into the shadows under the trees.

Zaki watched until every last trace of his friend's shaggy outline was gone.

"Goodbye," he whispered. "Now you can be a real bear!"

Zaki sat down, dazed and shaky. His time as a parent of bears was finally done. Now he had only his own survival and his own future to think about. He glanced about him at the other flotsam that the storm had washed up. There was his saucepan – dented, but still in one piece. And there was that box – his father's gift! Well, if it contained some horrid, shiny shirt, that might at least be useful, since the river had taken everything but his shorts.

Zaki frayed the string with a pebble and found a box within a box, and inside that, not a shirt but …

a flute. It was a real musician's flute, miraculously unharmed by all that had happened to it. He sat on the mud and played his beloved bears one last farewell.

Epilogue

Naz ran into the family compound, her plaits flying and her schoolbag slipping off her shoulder. "Zaki! Zaki! He's here!"

Zaki stared at her over a stack of wooden bed frames that he was moving into his mother's workshop. "Who's here? What are you talking about, Naz?"

"Raju Jayarman, of course," she said.

Zaki's heart skipped a few beats. Naz thrust a copy of a newspaper into his hands. Now he had been in school for almost two years, like Naz, reading was no longer a problem.

...the great Raju Jayarman is paying an unexpected visit to the city today. Before returning by sleeper train to the capital, he has agreed to give a recital in Plantation Park, this afternoon between 3 and 5...

"But it's already four, Naz." Zaki's face fell. "By the time I get there, it'll be over."

"What does that matter?" Naz exclaimed. "The

point is that *he* hears *you*, not that you hear him!"

Before Zaki could tell Naz that she was crazy, Rashma and Taroob had joined in the conversation, calling out through the workshop window.

"She's right, Zaki," Taroob said. "Get over there and show him how great your playing is now."

"I'll ring your father's mobile," Rashma said. "He can take you in the taxi."

"No need to call!" Tareef announced, hurrying into the compound. "I saw the paper and I was on my way to fetch the boy!" Tareef grinned at his son. "Leave those beds to the women! Get your instrument and we'll go."

Tareef's little green taxi had the words "Dancing Bear Rehabilitation Project" displayed on its side. In spite of his forebodings, Tareef had found that he rather liked driving a taxi. His passengers got a story with every journey and he was popular with visitors from out of town. He liked it so much that he wasn't at all cross that Zaki had run off with the cubs. In fact, he felt rather guilty, so when Zaki had returned, there was only delight to welcome him.

"Flute playing," Tareef had said, not long afterwards, "could be said to be a Kalandar tradition!"

But today, Tareef's new-found knowledge of side streets and shortcuts was not going to cut through the traffic. They were stuck in a jam. Every light was red; every road clogged with cars. They were still five blocks away from Plantation Park at half-past five. Zaki was almost relieved. He wouldn't hear the great man play, but he wouldn't have to suffer the humiliation of being pushed aside by his entourage. What did his family think? That you could just walk up to someone and play? It was mad. He stared at the red light ahead and said nothing.

But Tareef was looking at him. "Son," he said, "I have an idea. But it will mean you'll have to play in quite an unusual place. Could you do that?"

Cautiously, Zaki nodded.

"Don't ask any questions. Just do what I say. And," Tareef added with a wicked grin, "hold tight!"

Tareef drove onto the pavement like a movie stunt driver and ten minutes later brought the taxi to a screaming halt in front of a small blue door at the back of the train station. Tareef jumped out and after two minutes of conversation with the uniformed man at the door, he gestured urgently at Zaki to come.

"Go with this man," Tareef said, "and when he says play, play like your life depended on it."

The man moved quickly for someone so small and round. He raced through a maze of corridors and up a steep metal staircase into a room with an ancient microphone and a bank of switches on the wall.

"Quick!" said the man. "The sleeper to Dehli has just been called. If you play when I flip that red switch he will hear you. But you must never tell a soul I helped you!"

Flustered, nervous, no, *terrified*, Zaki stood before the microphone with his flute.

"Now!" said the man and flicked the switch.

No going back. Now or never.

All the times in the forest when his life and those of the cubs had depended on acting not thinking flashed through Zaki's brain. He stilled his pulse. He calmed his mind. He *breathed*.

And then ... he played. He played the birds calling in the dawn; the stars blazing; the tiger bursting orange from the grass; the sunlight through the fig trees; and the two greatest partings of his young life, one tragic and one triumphant.

Down on the station concourse, the great Raju Jayarman insisted that they held the sleeper for him until he found the musician whose flute-playing had made him weep and begged that person to come and work with him.

Back in the taxi, Tareef didn't dare to ask what had happened. He took his son's silence as a bad sign and tried to be kind. As they passed the offices of the Bear Project on Lake Road, he said, "That reminds me! Guess who I had in the taxi today?"

This was Tareef's new favourite phrase.

"I don't know," said Zaki quietly. "Who?"

"Mr Ahmed!" Tareef said. "He told me Bilqis is doing well and I told him about the cubs and about the brave things you did. He was very impressed. Did you know that there are professionals employed to do such work, teaching cubs that have been captured to live in the wild? They even have a special name for it. They call it *Walking the Bear*. It could be the career for you, son!"

Zaki smiled to himself. Tareef had grown truly proud of his son's flute playing, but still he felt that bears in *some* form *must* be his family's destiny.

"If the flute-playing doesn't work out, Father," he said sweetly, "I'll think about it."

Then Zaki closed his eyes, holding his joy inside like a secret fire and thinking of Lallu somewhere out there, being a real bear.

LIVING WITH BEARS

There's something about bears that human beings have always liked. Perhaps it's their ability to stand upright on their back legs the way we do. Whatever it is, bears have been the stars of myths and stories around the world and were believed to have all sorts of magical powers.

This has not been good news for real bears. Bears of several different species have been killed so that parts of their bodies can be made into "cures" for all sorts of diseases, and live cubs have been captured to be kept as pets or as performing animals. Captive brown bears, made to stand on their hind legs and "dance", were a popular entertainment all over Europe four hundred years ago, and there were still a handful in Eastern Europe up to 2007.

In India, the shaggy-coated sloth bear is the hero Jambavan of Hindu and Indian mythology, and the character Baloo from Rudyard Kipling's *The Jungle Book*. For hundreds of years, sloth bears were used by members of the Kalandar community as dancing bears. Kalandars were poor and semi-nomadic and depended on their dancing bears to make a living. Cubs, usually twins, would be taken from the den where they were born, when they were just a few weeks old. Often mother bears were killed when they tried to protect their cubs.

An ex-keeper holds up a photo taken on the day one Kalandar family gave up their bears

102

Cubs would then be raised by a Kalandar family and when they were just a few months old, their big canine teeth would be pulled out, to make them less dangerous, and a hole made in their noses with a heated spike. For the rest of their lives, these captive bears had a rope through that hole, to keep them under control and make them "dance". More than 200 cubs were being taken from the wild every year, and a third of these died because of the treatment they received in captivity. This practice was not only cruel, it was also reducing the numbers of wild sloth bears that were already under threat from habitat loss. This had a knock-on effect for the habitats where wild bears live, as they have an important role to play in dispersing the seeds of trees in their droppings.

Keeping dancing bears was made illegal in India in 1998, but it was still going on away from big towns and cities. Wildlife and animal welfare organizations, like Wildlife Trust of India (WTI) and the World Society for the Protection of Animals (WSPA) saw that the way to help sloth bears was to help the Kalandars to find other ways of making a living. So in 2005, WTI and WSPA began a project (SBCWP — Sloth Bear Conservation and Welfare Project) to win the trust of wary Kalandar communities and offer them help to change, in return for giving up their bears. The SBCWP gave Kalandar families money to start new businesses, to pay to educate their children and to train women who had never

This Kalandar community no longer depends on dancing bears for their livelihoods

worked outside their homes before. Families no longer had to travel from place to place to find new audiences for their bears; they could settle down and build new and better lives.

The project has been incredibly successful. Kalandar families all over India have made a new start and have a source of income that doesn't depend on bears, while their children can get an education. One Kalandar father that I met proudly told me that his daughter was going to become a doctor.

But what about the bears? Adult sloth bears who have had their teeth removed and have lived as captives on the end of a rope all their lives, can never return to the wild. But their damaged noses and teeth can be treated and they can live in sanctuaries where they can climb, dig and snuffle about and have some of the experiences of being a wild bear.

Returning cubs to the wild — if they still have their canine teeth — is possible, but very difficult. Sloth bear cubs live with their mother for two or even three years, learning from her about how to find food and stay safe

Retired adult sloth bears are cared for in animal sanctuaries

from predators, natural hazards and other bears. Sloth bears' lips and noses are adapted for feeding on ants and termites, but they also eat a wide variety of other foods, including many kinds of fruits and seeds and also honey. There's an awful lot for a cub to learn and it often happens that one of each pair of twins just doesn't make it.

For a human, taking on the role of mother bear is a huge task, but WTI, with help from another animal-welfare organization — International Fund for Animal Welfare — have a project called *Walking The Bear*, which does just that. Experienced wildlife rangers take cubs out into the wild to support and protect them while they learn how to be wild bears, as they would have done with their mothers. This has been done most successfully with Asian black bears, which are taken from the wild as cubs for the trade in bear body parts, but a few sloth bear cubs have also made it back to the wild this way.

The battle for the survival of sloth bears in the wild isn't over. In some areas of India and other parts of Southeast Asia, all sorts of cubs — sloth bears, Asian black bears, brown bears and sun bears — are still taken from the wild for the trade in bear body parts. Sloth bears face another problem in India. As their wild habitat is lost, they raid human crops for food and come into conflict with people; bears can end up attacking humans and, of course, humans then want to kill them.

Luckily, WTI and its partners are trying to resolve these conflicts and are helping to preserve wild spaces where bears can go on being bears.

You can help by telling people about the threats that bears face and by supporting conservation and animal-welfare organizations like WTI, IFAW and WSPA.

THE LION WHO STOLE MY ARM
Mozambique, Africa

Pedru hopes he's strong enough to kill the lion
who took his arm. But will he have the strength to
turn his back on revenge?